Charge of the
'hree-Horned Monster

D0263747

NEATH PORT TALBOT LIBRARIES

Dinosaur Cove™

A Cretaceous Adventure

Dinosaur Cove™

Charge of the
Three-Horned Monster

by
REX STONE

illustrated by
MIKE SPOOR

Series created by
Working Partners Ltd

OXFORD
UNIVERSITY PRESS

NEATH PORT TALBOT
LIBRARIES

2000606309

PETERS	06-Mar-2013
JF	£4.99
CYm	

For J_____ _____ and _____ _____ 'ho have

Specia_____ _____ _____ _____ _____ h Vogler

OXFORD
UNIVERSITY PRESS

Great Clarendon Street, Oxford OX2 6DP
Oxford University Press is a department of the University of Oxford.
It furthers the University's objective of excellence in research, scholarship,
and education by publishing worldwide in

Oxford   New York

Auckland   Cape Town   Dar es Salaam   Hong Kong   Karachi
Kuala Lumpur   Madrid   Melbourne   Mexico City   Nairobi
New Delhi   Shanghai   Taipei   Toronto

With offices in

Argentina   Austria   Brazil   Chile   Czech Republic   France   Greece
Guatemala   Hungary   Italy   Japan   Poland   Portugal   Singapore
South Korea   Switzerland   Thailand   Turkey   Ukraine   Vietnam

Oxford is a registered trade mark of Oxford University Press
in the UK and in certain other countries

© Working Partners Limited 2008
Illustrations © Mike Spoor 2008
Folio images pages 22-91 copyright © Ragnarok Press 2008

Series created by Working Partners Ltd

Dinosaur Cove is a registered trademark of Working Partners Ltd

The moral rights of the author have been asserted

Database right Oxford University Press (maker)

First published 2008
First published in this edition 2013

All rights reserved. No part of this publication may be reproduced,
stored in a retrieval system, or transmitted, in any form or by any means,
without the prior permission in writing of Oxford University Press,
or as expressly permitted by law, or under terms agreed with the appropriate
reprographics rights organization. Enquiries concerning reproduction
outside the scope of the above should be sent to the Rights Department,
Oxford University Press, at the address above

You must not circulate this book in any other binding or cover
and you must impose this same condition on any acquirer

British Library Cataloguing in Publication Data

Data available

ISBN: 978-0-19-279366-9

1 3 5 7 9 10 8 6 4 2

Printed in Italy

Paper used in the production of this book is a natural,
recyclable product made from wood grown in sustainable forests
The manufacturing process conforms to the environmental
regulations of the country of origin

FACT FILE

➡ JAMIE HAS JUST MOVED FROM THE CITY TO LIVE IN THE LIGHTHOUSE IN DINOSAUR COVE. JAMIE'S DAD IS OPENING A DINOSAUR MUSEUM ON THE BOTTOM FLOOR OF THE LIGHTHOUSE. WHEN JAMIE GOES HUNTING FOR FOSSILS IN THE CRUMBLING CLIFFS ON THE BEACH HE MEETS A LOCAL BOY, TOM, AND THE TWO DISCOVER AN AMAZING SECRET: A WORLD WITH **REAL, LIVE DINOSAURS!** BUT IT'S NOT ONLY DINOSAURS THAT INHABIT THIS PREHISTORIC WORLD...

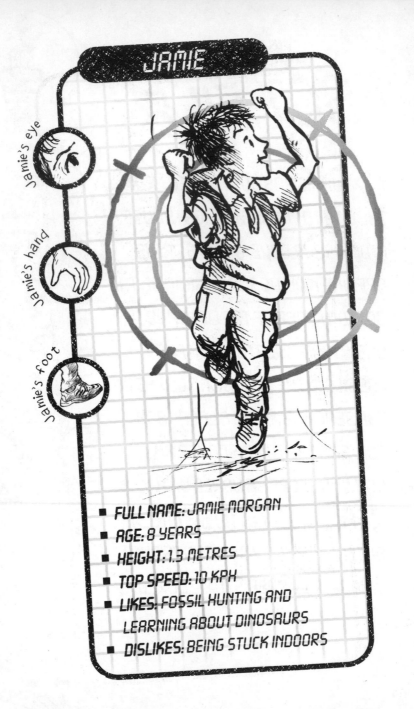

JAMIE

Jamie's eye

Jamie's hand

Jamie's foot

- **FULL NAME:** JAMIE MORGAN
- **AGE:** 8 YEARS
- **HEIGHT:** 1.3 METRES
- **TOP SPEED:** 10 KPH
- **LIKES:** FOSSIL HUNTING AND LEARNING ABOUT DINOSAURS
- **DISLIKES:** BEING STUCK INDOORS

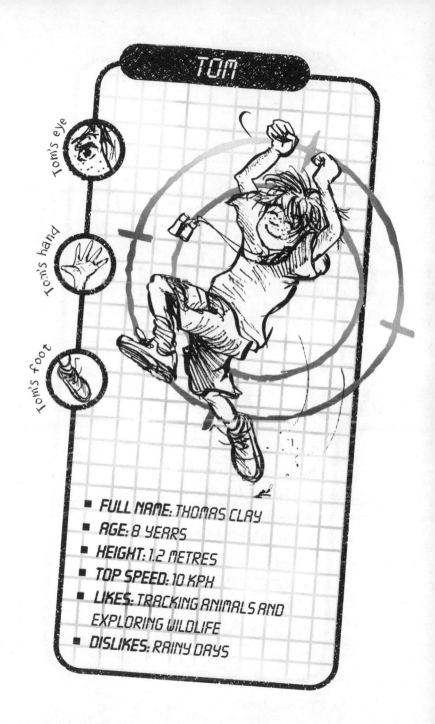

TOM

Tom's eye

Tom's hand

Tom's foot

- **FULL NAME:** THOMAS CLAY
- **AGE:** 8 YEARS
- **HEIGHT:** 1.2 METRES
- **TOP SPEED:** 10 KPH
- **LIKES:** TRACKING ANIMALS AND EXPLORING WILDLIFE
- **DISLIKES:** RAINY DAYS

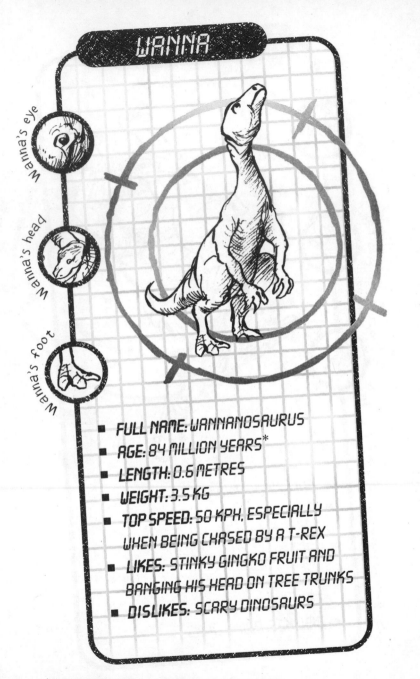

WANNA

wanna's eye

wanna's head

wanna's foot

- **FULL NAME:** WANNANOSAURUS
- **AGE:** 84 MILLION YEARS*
- **LENGTH:** 0.6 METRES
- **WEIGHT:** 3.5 KG
- **TOP SPEED:** 50 KPH, ESPECIALLY WHEN BEING CHASED BY A T-REX
- **LIKES:** STINKY GINGKO FRUIT AND BANGING HIS HEAD ON TREE TRUNKS
- **DISLIKES:** SCARY DINOSAURS

*__NOTE:__ SCIENTISTS CALL THIS PERIOD THE LATE CRETACEOUS

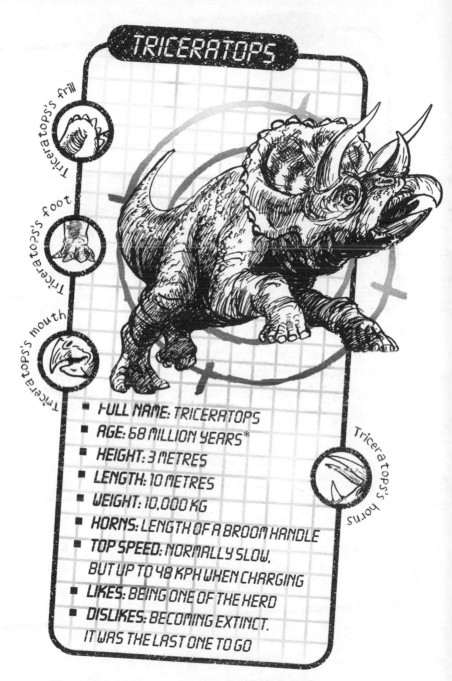

TRICERATOPS

Triceratops's frill

Triceratops's foot

Triceratops's mouth

Triceratops's horns

- **FULL NAME:** TRICERATOPS
- **AGE:** 68 MILLION YEARS*
- **HEIGHT:** 3 METRES
- **LENGTH:** 10 METRES
- **WEIGHT:** 10,000 KG
- **HORNS:** LENGTH OF A BROOM HANDLE
- **TOP SPEED:** NORMALLY SLOW, BUT UP TO 48 KPH WHEN CHARGING
- **LIKES:** BEING ONE OF THE HERD
- **DISLIKES:** BECOMING EXTINCT. IT WAS THE LAST ONE TO GO

*__NOTE:__ SCIENTISTS CALL THIS PERIOD THE LATE CRETACEOUS

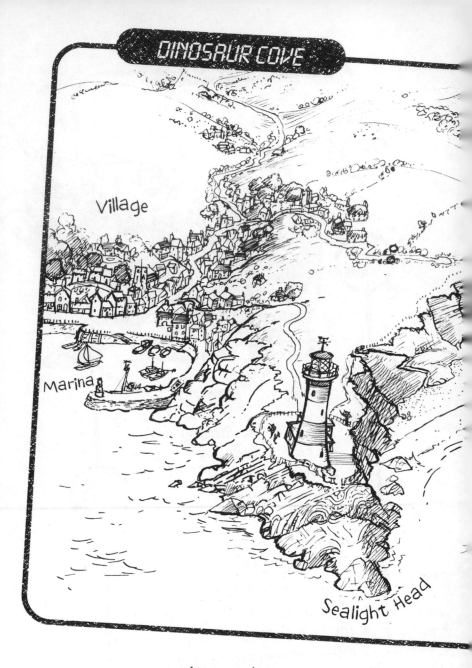

DINOSAUR COVE

Village

Marina

Sealight Head

Landslips where clay and fossils are

Muddy beach

DINO CAVE

High Tide beach line

Low Tide beach line

Sea

Smuggler's Point

CHAPTER 1

Jamie Morgan sprinted along the
pebbly beach of Dinosaur Cove to
meet his new best friend.

'Have you got everything?' asked
Tom Clay, jumping off the rock
he was standing on. 'I brought my
binoculars and my compass.'

Jamie took off
his backpack and
rummaged inside
for his fossil hunting
equipment. 'I've got
my pocket knife, my
notebook, and the
Fossil Finder.' Jamie's
brand new hand-held
computer had all
sorts of prehistoric
information at the
touch of a few buttons.
'I brought some
sandwiches, too,'
Jamie said. 'Cheese

and Grandad's home-made pickle.
It'll blow your head off!'

'I can't wait to get back to our cave,'
Tom said, hopping from one foot to
another.

'You mean you can't wait to get
back to the dinosaurs!' Jamie said,
as the two friends hurried down the
beach. Jamie had met Tom for the
first time yesterday and together
they had discovered Dinosaur
Cove's biggest secret: an amazing
world of living dinosaurs!
First, Jamie had found a
set of fossilized dinosaur
footprints, and then the

footprints had transported them to a place where dinosaurs still roamed the earth.

'It's hard keeping something so big a secret,' Tom confessed. 'My big brother kept asking me what I did yesterday.'

'I know!' Jamie replied. 'My dad got a huge triceratops skull fossil for the museum this morning, and I kept thinking about the *real* triceratops we saw yesterday.'

Jamie and his dad had moved in with his grandad to the old lighthouse on the cliffs and Jamie's dad planned to open a dinosaur museum on the ground floor. Jamie's dad knew more about dinosaurs than anyone, but he didn't know the colours of a t-rex like Jamie and Tom did!

'I forgot to tell you!' panted Jamie, as they scrambled up the steep path towards their secret cave. 'I brought some coloured pencils with me. I thought we could make a map of Dino World in my notebook.'

'Good idea,' Tom said. 'We'll be like real explorers, charting unknown territories!'

'And seeing lots of dinosaurs!'

They reached the tall stack of boulders that led to their secret cave, and climbed up using cracks in the rock. From the top of the boulders, Jamie could see his grandad fishing for lobster out in the cove.

Jamie quickly
slipped into the
dark cave, but
Tom paused at the
hidden entrance.
'What if Dino
World's not there?'
he asked. 'What if we
dreamt it?'

Jamie laughed, and the sound
echoed around the cave. 'No way!
That t-rex we met was definitely
real!' With a shiver of excitement he
turned on his torch and shone it into
the far corner. The beam picked out
the small gap in the cave wall.

Jamie took off his backpack and crawled through on his belly into the second chamber which was narrower and pitch dark. Jamie and Tom suspected they were the only people ever to have been in this place.

Jamie flashed his torch over the stone floor. 'Here are the fossilized dinosaur footprints we found yesterday.'

'The best fossil anyone has ever found!' Tom said. The footprints had somehow transported the boys to Dino World.

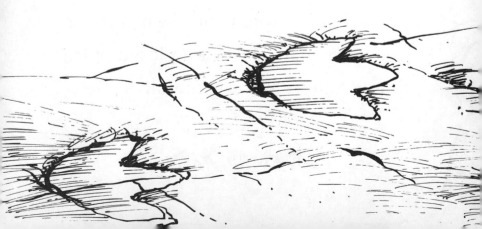

Tom stepped into the first clover-shaped indent in the cave floor. 'Here goes!' He placed his foot carefully into each footprint, walking in the dinosaur tracks.

Jamie stuck close behind him and counted every step. 'One . . . two . . . three . . . four . . . FIVE!'

In an instant, the cold, damp cave was gone and Jamie and Tom were standing in a bright sunny cave and staring out at giant, sun-dappled trees.

The air was hot and humid and they could hear the heavy drone of insects. They ran out on to the damp squelchy ground of Dino World.

'We're back in the jungle,' said Jamie happily. 'We're on Gingko Hill.'

'This is so cool!' said Tom, looking eagerly around.

Jamie laughed. 'Boiling, you mean!' He picked a large leaf off the ground and fanned himself. Suddenly he stopped. 'What was that?'

The boys listened hard. From somewhere in the steaming jungle they could hear scuffling—and it was getting nearer.

'Something's coming!' warned Tom.

Just then, a plump, scaly little creature with a flat, bony head burst out from a clump of ferns. It scuttled along on its stumpy hind legs and hurled itself at Jamie, knocking him flat on his back.

Grunk! *Grunk!* *Grunk!*

'It's Wanna!' exclaimed Tom in relief.

Jamie and Tom had met the wannanosaurus on their first visit to Dino World, and the Fossil Finder had said that it was pronounced 'wah-nan-oh-sor-us'. Wanna had helped them when the t-rex was after them and turned out to be a true friend.

'Stop licking, Wanna!' panted Jamie, trying to push him off. 'Your tongue's like sandpaper.'

Tom reached up to a nearby gingko tree and picked a handful of the small, foul-smelling fruit. He held one out. 'Have a stink-o bomb, Wanna. Your favourite!'

Wanna bounded over and greedily gobbled it up as Jamie staggered to his feet. Tom gave him one more and then quickly tossed a few more pieces of the fruit to Jamie, who hid them in his backpack.

'Let's start mapping!' said Tom.

Wanna sniffed the bag as Jamie dug around and pulled out his notebook and coloured pencils. 'We're here,' he said, drawing Gingko Hill in the middle of the page.

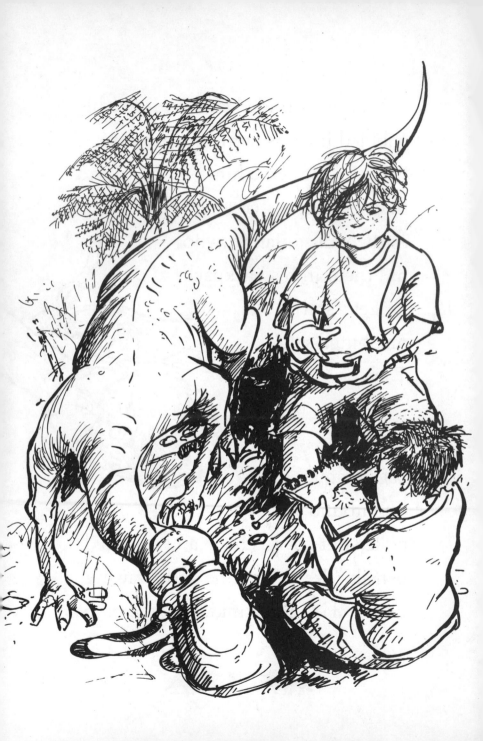

'Yesterday we found the ocean and the lagoon in the west.' He sketched them in.

Tom checked the compass. 'So let's head north today.'

'Great,' said Jamie. 'Come on, Wanna! We're going exploring.'

Wanna wagged his tail and trotted happily alongside the boys. They scrambled through ferns and creepers and squelched among slimy giant toadstools.

At last they came to a break in the trees and peered through. Below was the dense tangle of the jungle and beyond that vast grassy plains

with a wide river
snaking through towards
their hill.

'Look at those far away
mountains,' said Tom,
scanning the horizon

 28

with the binoculars. 'They're so
high their peaks are hidden in
the clouds.'

'Far Away Mountains—that's a
good name!' said Jamie, and scribbled
it down on the map.

 29

Then Jamie took the binoculars and scanned the plains, and what he saw made him gasp. There were about fifteen strange-looking houses made of orange earth sitting near a curve in the river.

'What is it?' Tom asked.

'I don't know,' Jamie replied. 'I think . . . I think there's a village!'

'No way!' Tom said. He grabbed the binoculars and gasped. 'I thought we were the only people in Dino World.'

'Me too,' said Jamie. 'But . . . who could they be? There weren't any people around during dinosaur times.

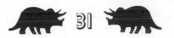

Humans didn't come along for millions of years!'

'Well, if *we're* here,' Tom reasoned, 'maybe other people got through too?'

'Or maybe the houses aren't for people at all, but something else,' Jamie guessed, as he added this odd discovery to his map. 'How should I label it?'

'I'm not sure,' Tom admitted. 'Since we don't know what they are, we need to investigate. That's what real explorers would do!'

Following Tom's compass, the two boys set off north-east down the

rest of
Gingko
Hill. Wanna
made excited
grunks as he clambered
over roots and ferns. The
trunks of giant trees rose into
the misty canopy and insects
as big and colourful as
parrots buzzed around
their heads. Soon they
heard splashing and found
themselves on the banks of a
wide river that cut the forest
in two.

'We'll have to swim it if we're going to get to those houses,' Tom said as he started down the bank.

'Wait!' warned Jamie, peeling off his backpack and pulling out his Fossil Finder. He flipped open the lid. On the screen a picture of a t-rex footprint glowed and above it the words, *'HAPPY HUNTING'*. A cursor blinked at the bottom

and Jamie tapped in the keywords: *PREHISTORIC RIVER CREATURES.*

'We might meet one of these,' he said, handing the Fossil Finder to Tom. '*CHAMPSOSAURUS*,' read Tom. 'Hmm. Looks like a crocodile.'

'And we'd look like its dinner!' Jamie peered into the water for signs of life and spotted several greyish humps. 'Look over there.'

'Those are stones, fossil-brain,' Tom said. 'We can cross there!'

When the three of them reached the other side, Tom checked his compass again and they headed off through the trees.

'How long
do you think it'll
take us to get to the houses?'
Tom asked.

'Hard to tell,' puffed Jamie.
'But we've got to figure out what
those things are for our map.'

The boys stumbled into a
large clearing surrounded by
three walls of creepers. Spiky
plants grew all over the
ground, and Wanna

grabbed a clump in his mouth and
chomped happily.

'OK, Wanna. Lunchtime!' declared
Jamie. He climbed onto a log and tore
the tinfoil off the cheese and pickle
sandwiches. He was just handing a
sandwich to Tom when Wanna leapt
up and grabbed half of it in his mouth.

'Hey, that's my lunch!' exclaimed
Tom. Wanna chewed greedily.
Suddenly, the little dinosaur blinked
in surprise and began to run around
in circles, shaking his head and
making strange gak-gak noises.

'He's discovered Grandad's pickle!'
Jamie laughed.

A deep rumbling sound from the forest made Jamie and Tom instantly stop laughing.

'Only something really big could make that noise,' murmured Tom, glancing over his shoulder. 'What if it's the t-rex again?'

'Wait—I can hear mooing,' said Jamie, puzzled. His attention was fixed on the wall of creepers nearest to them.

'Like a herd of giant cows,' said Tom.

There was a sound of snapping and splitting vines. Jamie and Tom leapt to their feet as the creepers just

in front of them
began to shake. Jamie
dropped his sandwich
as the last strands tore
away.

A massive beaked
head with three huge
horns peered into the
clearing.

CHAPTER 3

'It's a triceratops!' whispered Jamie, transfixed by the giant head looming above him.

'Awesome!'

Jamie and Tom could feel its hot breath on their faces. With a snort,

the dinosaur forced its body through the creepers and took a lumbering step into the clearing.

'I'm glad it's not a t-rex,' Tom said. 'But I can't believe it's so gigantic!'

'Dad was telling me about triceratops this morning,' said Jamie. 'It weighs about ten thousand kilos— the same as the largest elephant ever!'

'I don't want that treading on my toes!' Tom hastily scrambled onto the log and pulled Jamie up behind him.

The creepers shook again and another triceratops pushed its way into the clearing. Soon a whole

herd of the three-horned creatures
stomped into view.

One t-tops put his head down to eat
some of the spiky grass right in front
of them. The herd munched on the
grass, completely ignoring the boys.

'Look, Wanna!' Jamie said, as their
dinosaur friend gobbled up a flower

nearby. 'They're herbivores, like you, which means they won't want to eat us.'

'That's true, but if one steps on us, it would be just as dangerous!' replied Tom. 'We'd better not risk trying to walk through them. Maybe we should try to scare them away from the clearing?'

'I don't think scaring a herd of triceratops would be a good idea,' Jamie said. 'They might end up charging like a herd of elephants!'

They heard a lowing from the
biggest dinosaur in the herd. The
sound rumbled around the clearing
as the others took up the call.
It shook the boys on their log.

'The leader's given a signal,' Tom
said. 'What does it mean?'

'I think it means they're moving

on!' said Jamie. 'And they're going in
the direction of the houses.'

The boys tried to keep their
balance as their log was bumped from
all sides by the tree trunk-sized legs
going by, but it was too much! Jamie
slipped off the log and had to roll
away quickly to avoid being trampled.

'What are we going to do?'
Jamie said, breathlessly, as he
scrambled safely back onto the
log. 'We've got to get away from
their feet!'

'It seems to me that the safest
place is on top of a t-tops!' Tom said.
'Otherwise, we'll be squished!'

'Fossil-brain!' squeaked Jamie.
'We would need a trampoline to get
up there.'

'Maybe we don't,' Tom said.
He pulled some gingkoes out of
Jamie's bag and held one out. One
of the beasts stopped and sniffed
the air. Then it turned its head to

face the boys, and gave a blasting snort that nearly blew the boys off the log. Tom quickly dropped the gingko onto the ground. The beast lowered its gigantic head and its frill was in their reach. Its powerful jaws ground noisily as it chewed the orange fruit.

Tom tossed several other gingkoes onto the ground and whispered, 'Now, we can try to climb on board.'

Tom quickly took hold of the frill and pulled himself onto the triceratops's forehead, being careful not to frighten it. Then he reached down and gave Jamie a hand up.

Soon they were both sitting on the leathery neck and holding on to one of the triceratops's horns.

'We're away from the huge legs, but what if it throws us off?' Jamie asked.

'I don't think it even noticed us,' Tom replied.

Their triceratops finished its gingkoes and then raised its head and began to follow the herd. Wanna stared up at them, his head on one side.

'Hey, Wanna,' waved Tom. 'Look at us!'

'This is awesome!' declared Jamie. 'It's like being on the handlebars of a giant bike.'

'Hold tight for a bumpy ride,' said Tom.

The dinosaur swayed as it plodded steadily through the tangle of jungle creepers and trees. Jamie and Tom slid about, dodging the passing branches

while Wanna trotted among the legs
of the herd, grunking at the top of
his voice.

'This is much faster than walking!'
Jamie laughed.

Suddenly the boys could see bright
light through the giant leaves and
branches. The herd left the jungle
behind and lumbered out into the
dazzling sunlight of the plains.

CHAPTER 4

Jamie squinted at the open land
shimmering in the heat.

'Look!' He pointed. 'There's the
river again—it comes down from
the mountains.' He leaned his
notebook on the triceratops's horn

and drew a winding line from the mountain peaks across the plains to the jungle.

'In a way, we're the first people ever to make a map,' said Tom as the herd moved steadily across the sweltering plains.

'The first explorers, riding out on safari,' declared Jamie, laughing. 'This is great. I can see for miles!'

'Look at all these fantastic dinosaurs,' Tom said. He pointed to a slow-moving herd grazing on the leaves of some trees and spoke to an imaginary camera. 'This is Tom Clay, reporting live from Dino World, on

the Great Plains. Who needs a jeep when you have the luxury of T-Tops Travel?'

Jamie laughed. He knew Tom wanted to be a famous wildlife presenter one day.

Tom went on. 'Here we are watching the alamosaurs reaching their long necks to the highest branches, and further in the distance we can see the strange dwellings that we are about to investigate. Stay tuned for what could be the most exciting discovery of all time!'

The t-tops lumbered on as the boys watched the scenery go by.

'Can you see that weird rock there?' said Tom, checking his compass. 'Over to the east.'

'It looks like a huge fang,' Jamie said. 'Let's call it Fang Rock!' He drew in the pointy rock and labelled it. Then he looked up. 'Hey, we're really close to the houses now.' He hurriedly put his notebook away. 'They're at least three times as tall as my dad!'

The thin towers stood in a silent group in the baking heat, silent and seemingly uninhabited.

'I don't think they are houses,' said Jamie. The mounds were made out of

bumpy orange dirt
and had deep crevices
running down them.
There weren't any
windows or doors,
and Jamie couldn't
imagine what kind
of creature could live
in them.

'There's no sign
of any dinosaurs,'
said Tom. 'This feels
weird.'

'As if something's
waiting to happen,'
Jamie whispered.

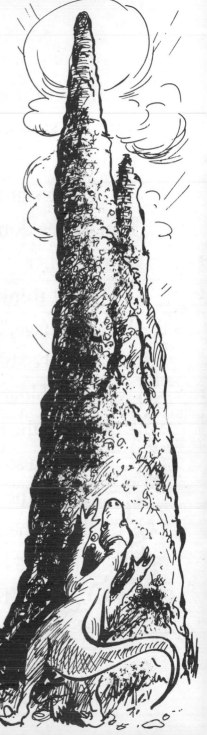

The herd stopped a little way from the strange towers and mooed anxiously.

'They're signalling again,' said Tom. 'They don't seem to like the towers either.'

'I don't think Wanna understands their language,' Jamie said.

Instead of being cautious, Wanna was scrabbling excitedly at the bottom of one of the towers. All of a sudden, a stream of orange insects was pouring out of the hole and all over the little dinosaur. Wanna jumped back, batting at his face with his claws.

'Termites!'
gasped Tom. 'These are
termite mounds.'
The ant-like
creatures were as
big as mice and Jamie
had never seen anything
like them.

Wanna was yelping and shaking
himself as they crawled all over him.

'Wanna is too quick for them,'
said Jamie, as the little dinosaur
did a frantic dance. 'He's flinging
them off with all that jerking
around!'

'But he's scaring the triceratops!'
Tom cried.

The triceratops stamped their
feet in alarm and backed off,
jostling each other. The shaking
of the earth seemed to wake the
termites and thousands of them
poured out of every mound.
Jamie saw the bugs stream up the
legs of the leader of the herd and
into its eyes and nose.

The leader tossed its head like an angry bull to shake the insects off but it was no use. It couldn't move as easily as small, agile Wanna. Suddenly it bellowed in terror and charged straight through the termite city! Dry dirt and insects scattered everywhere.

Jamie and Tom felt their t-tops lurching forward, as the other dinosaurs began to run.

'It's a stampede!' yelled Jamie. 'Hold on!'

The boys clung to the horns as the herd took off through the cloud of orange dust. Jamie felt like a rodeo

rider being bucked about. Then he felt a prickle on his leg and looked down to see a termite crawling on him. Despite the bumping, Jamie managed to flick it away quickly. But soon, a whole army of termites was crawling over their t-tops's head towards him.

Jamie tried to knock away the ones that crawled onto him, but all the movement made his backpack slip from his shoulder! He flung out an arm to catch it as it fell, but it was too late. Jamie's backpack tumbled to the ground and disappeared beneath the cloud of dust.

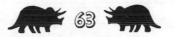

Jamie couldn't believe it. He had lost his precious Fossil Finder and his notebook and there was nothing he could do about it.

Insects were scuttling all over him now, crawling in his hair and down his neck. 'Yow!' Jamie wailed as one termite bit him on the leg. Pain shot right down to his foot, but he managed to flick another termite away.

'I've been bitten, too!' cried Tom.

The boys tried to ignore the horrible itching and just clung on for dear life.

'Where's Wanna?' yelled Tom.

'I don't know,' Jamie shouted. 'I can't see him!'

The stampede rushed forward and all at once the herd plunged downwards.

'We're going down the riverbank!' Tom leaned back and gripped tightly as they approached the water.

Jamie gulped. 'And we're not stopping!'

SPLASH!

Their triceratops plunged into the
churning river. The boys were thrown
into the water among the giant
thrashing dinosaurs and drowning

insects. Jamie swam up to the surface
and held his hands out, keeping
him away from the dinosaurs'
bodies and horns.

The huge dinosaurs stood in the
water, seemingly relieved that the
biting termites were being swept
away by the river.

'They wanted to wash the
termites off,' Jamie managed
to splutter.

'And us too!' Tom replied.
The boys felt the pull of the
river and soon were sucked
into the current.

'Thanks for the ride!' Jamie called out as they left their triceratops taxi far behind.

Jamie heard a grunking noise nearby. 'Wanna!' he cried. The little dinosaur was running along the riverbank trying to keep pace with them and he had something in his mouth.

'Your backpack!' Tom exclaimed. 'It's safe!'

'Go, Wanna!' shouted Jamie.

Jamie and Tom were both good swimmers but the current was too strong to let them swim to the edge. When a log swept by, Jamie

and Tom grabbed on to its stubby
branches.

'Phew,' gasped Tom as he got a
good hold. He checked out the river
ahead. 'Do you think there are any
champsosaurs in here?'

'I hope not,' Jamie groaned. 'I
think we've met enough prehistoric
beasts for one day.'

The boys' log floated
into a patch of
shadow and
Tom looked
up. 'It's
Fang Rock!'
he said.

'We must be going towards Gingko
Hill—and home!'

'Maybe it will take us all the
way back, and save us the walk.'
Jamie grinned.

The river twisted round Fang Rock
and out again into the sunshine.
They could see Wanna on the bank.
He was jumping up and down and
grunking excitedly.

'What's the matter with Wanna?' Tom wondered aloud.

Jamie heard the sound of rushing water, and soon the boys' log was being knocked this way and that between sharp rocks. The water churned and bubbled, and Jamie realized that he could see the river ahead of them disappear. The land on either side of the river fell away and Jamie realized what Wanna was trying to warn them about. 'It's a waterfall!'

The boys kicked frantically towards the bank but the current was too strong. The log bumped and spun on towards the dangerous drop. Just before the boys were about to go over, the log caught suddenly between two rocks. The boys only just managed to hold on as white water crashed over their shoulders.

'Phew!' exclaimed Jamie. He
could just see over the fall down
to a large swirling pool below and
was relieved that the log had saved
them. He gave Tom a wobbly smile.
'Let's get out of here.'

Creeeeak!

'What was that?' he gasped.

'The log's splitting from the
force of the current!' yelled Tom.

'We're going to go over the waterfall!'

Jamie caught at his arm. 'Take a deep breath when you fall!' he shouted urgently. 'Start swimming the moment you can!'

Crack!

The log broke and the boys were sucked through the white foaming water and over the edge.

'Aaaah!' Jamie shouted as he plummeted down and down.

He took a huge breath just in time.

SPLASH!

He hit the churning water and plunged under the surface, tumbling round and round. Jamie felt the waterfall pushing him to the bottom of the river. He opened his eyes but it was murky and dark and all he could see were bubbles swirling around him. He couldn't even tell which way up was.

Then his foot touched rock. He pushed away hard, kicking his legs for all they were worth. At last he was at the surface, gulping in the wonderful air. He swam around, looking for Tom. He hoped his friend was all right!

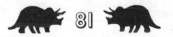

Suddenly, the water beside him erupted and Tom bobbed up like a cork, gasping for breath.

Jamie and Tom looked up in awe at the huge waterfall they had just come over. 'We made it!'

'A huge waterfall, an army of termites, a ride on a triceratops,' Tom said. 'Another great adventure in Dino World!'

The boys swam away from the waterfall and let the gentle current take them downstream. Ahead the river disappeared back into the jungle. The current swept them round to the right where the trees were dense and tangled with creepers.

The river now became wider and slower. With weak strokes, the boys made their way to the side and grabbed hold of an overhanging branch.

'I can touch the bottom,' gasped Tom. 'There's a ledge.'

They dragged themselves out of the water and collapsed on the safe, dry bank.

Grunk
    grunk!

Wanna bounded up and threw himself on them, licking and nudging them in turn. Then he disappeared into the undergrowth and came back a moment later with the backpack in his mouth. He dropped it in front of the boys.

Jamie sat up. 'He kept it safe! Well done, Wanna. You're a real mate.'

Tom reached over and got a gingko out of the bag. 'You deserve this!' he said, giving it to Wanna. The little dinosaur gobbled it down and gave Tom another huge lick.

'Yuck!' he cried, pushing him away. 'Stink-o breath!'

'Where are we?' asked Jamie.

'Well, you've got the map!' laughed Tom.

Jamie pulled it out and the boys had a look around. There was a steep slope ahead of them, covered in a thick wall of trees.

'I can just hear the waterfall,' said Tom. He got to his feet and peered

through the binoculars. 'Yes, it's back
there. It must be—look, there's the
point of Fang Rock.' He checked his
compass. 'It's east of here.'

They looked at their map.

'And the river comes from the
mountains in the north-east and
flows across the plains.' Jamie traced
it with his finger.

'Then it goes through the jungle here—where we are,' added Tom.

Jamie gazed at the trees ahead of them. 'Then we must be at the bottom of Gingko Hill. Told you it would save us the walk!'

Tom checked his watch. 'Lucky this is waterproof,' he grinned. 'It's not long before the tide comes in. We don't want to get trapped in the cliffs.'

Jamie nodded. 'Grandad will be back with his lobsters and he'll be wondering where we are.' He picked up his backpack. 'Who'd have thought making a map would be such an adventure?'

They climbed back up Gingko
Hill. As they passed the break in the
trees, Jamie looked back out over
the plains. He could see the termite
mounds in the distance, and
beyond that, on the other
side of the river, was the
grazing triceratops herd.
'Those termite bites

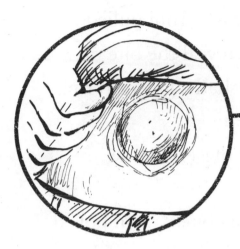

really hurt when we
got them,' said Jamie,
pulling up his trousers
to reveal a purple pus-filled bump
the size of an apricot. 'But they don't
really hurt any more.'

'Ew!' Tom crinkled up his nose. 'That looks so gross.' Tom pulled up his T-shirt to reveal the bite on his stomach that had a greenish ring around it.

'Yours is even bigger!' Jamie declared.

'Prehistoric bug bites.' Tom poked the squishy bump which seemed ready to pop at any minute. 'We'd better not let our parents see these! We'd never be able to explain them.'

Wanna bounded along with them but as they reached the entrance to the cave, he slowed down and lowered his head.

Grunk?

'See you, Wanna,' said Jamie,
patting him on his hard, flat head.
'We'll be back soon.'

'And that's a promise!' added
Tom. He pulled out the last two
gingko fruits.

Wanna wagged his tail and gobbled up his treat happily.

Jamie and Tom stepped into the cave. Jamie placed his feet in the dinosaur footprints and felt the ground get harder as he went. On his fifth step, he was plunged into inky darkness, and he was back in the cave in Dinosaur Cove. A moment later, Tom was standing next to him.

Jamie flicked on his torch and led the way out of the cave, down the rock fall, and back along the path to the beach.

'What an adventure!' said Tom.

'Better than any theme park,'

agreed Jamie. He fished out his notebook and flicked to the map. 'Look how far we travelled today! Right out on to the plains—and back the quick way!' He pointed to Fang Rock. 'The waterfall was just here. What shall we call it?'

'Crashing Rock Falls!' declared Tom.

'Cool! Maybe I'll draw us going over the edge.' Jamie grinned.

'Ahoy there, boys!' Grandad was rowing back towards the beach.

The boys waved and ran down to the sea.

'Come on,' he called. 'I can't land the boat without your help.'

Jamie and Tom jumped into the
surf and waded out to the boat,
helping Grandad pull the boat up
the beach.

'The moment we're done, Jamie,'
Grandad said as they unloaded the
full lobster pots, 'you must show
Tom the new triceratops skull.

95

It's sixty-eight million years old.'
He clapped Tom on the back. 'I bet
you haven't seen anything like that
before!'

Jamie and Tom smiled at each
other. Grandad would never believe
what they *had* seen today in Dino
World!

Far Away Mountains

Great Plains

Fang Rock

Crashing Rock Falls

Gingko Hill

GLOSSARY

Alamosaurus (al-am-oh-sor-us) – a gigantic dinosaur with a vegetarian diet that searched for food with its long neck and tiny head while protecting itself with its long, whip-like tail.

Champsosaurus (champ-so-sor-us) – crocodile-like prehistoric creature with a long, thin, tooth-filled snout, living and hunting in rivers and swamps.

Fossil – the remains or imprint of plants or animals found in rocks. They help scientists unravel the mysteries of prehistoric times.

Fossil Finder – hand-held computer filled with dinosaur facts.

Gingko (gink-oh) – a tree native to China called a 'living fossil' because fossils of it have been found dating back millions of years, yet they are still around today. Also known as the stink-bomb tree because of its smelly apricot-like fruit.

Herbivore – an animal that only eats plants;
a vegetarian.

Termite – ant-like insects that grow as big as mice
in Dino World. These prehistoric pests lived and
worked together to build orange house-high mounds
out of soil and spit, and there are still several kinds
of termites around today.

Triceratops (t-tops) (try-serra-tops) – a three-
horned, plant-eating dinosaur which looks like a
rhinoceros.

Tyrannosaurus Rex (t-rex) (ti-ran-oh-sor-us rex)
– a meat eating dinosaur with a huge tail, two
strong legs but two tiny arms. T-Rex was one of the
biggest and scariest dinosaurs.

Wannanosaurus (wah-nan-oh-sor-us) – a dinosaur
that only ate plants and used its hard, flat skull
to defend itself. Named after the place it was
discovered: Wannano in China.

Turn the page
to read the
first chapter of the
next adventure in the

Dinosaur Cove™

series:

March of the
Armoured Beasts

Jamie picked out a small fossil
from the heap of gooey mud that
had slipped down onto Dinosaur
Cove beach in the night. The stone
looked like a stubby pencil with
a sharp point. He wiped it on his

jeans and handed it to his best
friend Tom.

'That could be a dinosaur tooth,'
Jamie's grandad said, putting down
his fishing bucket and leaning in for
a closer look.

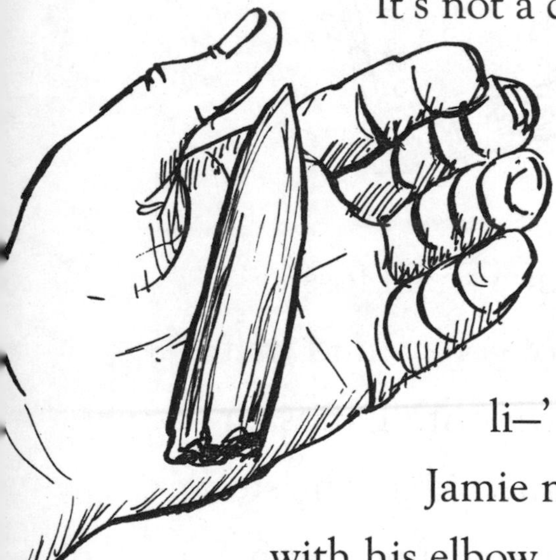

'It's not a dinosaur
tooth,' Tom
replied. 'They
don't look
anything like
this in real
li—'
Jamie nudged Tom
with his elbow. Grandad
didn't know they'd discovered real

live dinosaurs through a secret cave in Dinosaur Cove.

'Let's find out what it is.' Jamie rummaged inside his backpack. 'Compass . . . cheese and pickle sandwiches . . . Fossil Finder!' Jamie flipped open the lid of the hand-held computer and typed 'stubby pencil' in the search box. At once a picture of the fossil popped up.

'*BEL-EM-NITE*,' he read. '*THIS BULLET-SHAPED FOSSIL IS THE BODY OF A SEA CREATURE LIKE A SQUID.*' Jamie snapped the Fossil Finder shut and put it, and the belemnite, in his backpack.

'Fossil squid, eh?' Grandad chuckled. 'You can't eat those! I'm off to find some *fresh* fish.'

'And we should go find some fresh dinosaurs,' Tom whispered to Jamie as Grandad gathered up his fishing gear.

'Don't get stuck in the mud!' Grandad's eyes twinkled as he turned towards the sea. 'It'll swallow you up and spit out your bones, just like it did to the dinosaurs . . . '

The instant Grandad was out of hearing range, the boys yelled, 'Dino World here we come!'

They dashed towards the path that led from the beach up to the

smugglers' cave where the hidden
entrance to Dino World was. At the
bottom of the path, Jamie spotted
two large footprints in the sand.

Jamie skidded to a halt. 'Wait,
Tom. Someone has been here!'

Tom bent down to
examine the shoe
imprints. 'They're fresh,'
he said, 'and they're
leading up our
path!'

'Oh no,' Jamie
groaned.
'What if
someone's

found the way through our cave into
Dino World?'

'Then it wouldn't be our secret
any more,' Tom said grimly. 'You
know grown-ups. They'd sell tickets
to visitors to make money out of it.'

Jamie frowned. 'Or they'd say
it was dangerous and

close it up completely. We might
never get to go back!'

Jamie and Tom examined
the ground carefully
and followed the
footprints up

the
steep slope
to the pile of boulders
beneath their secret cave.
'Someone definitely came
this way,' Jamie said.
'We've got to make sure the cave's
safe.' He clambered up the boulders
as fast as he could.

'What are you waiting for?'
he called from the top. Tom was
lingering over a footprint beneath the
boulders. Jamie hopped impatiently
from one foot to another as Tom
scaled the boulders and hauled
himself up next to Jamie.

'There's no need to panic.' Tom
grinned and led the way into the cool
cave. 'No one came in here. Those
footprints went on past the boulders.
Our cave is safe!'

'But what if they come back?'
Jamie flicked on his torch and
shone it into the corner of the cave.
The light disappeared into the gap

they'd discovered on their
first visit.

'Stop worrying,' Tom
told him. 'There's no way
someone with feet that big
could get through here.'

'You're right.' Jamie
breathed a sigh of relief as
he pushed his backpack
through the tiny gap and
crawled in after it, followed
closely by Tom.

He flashed his torch
over the floor of the secret
chamber and picked out
the fossilized footprints of

their
dinosaur
friend,
Wanna, which
had led them twice
into Dino World.

'That foot wouldn't fit in these tracks, either.' Jamie stepped into the first of the small clover-shaped prints in the solid rock. 'But they're exactly the right size for us!'

'Then let's track dinosaurs!' Tom declared. 'I'm right behind you.'

'One . . . two . . . three . . . ' Jamie's heart beat faster as he counted each step. *What kind of dinosaurs will we see today?* he wondered.

'. . . four . . .'

The cave wall in front of him looked like solid rock, but as he put his foot forward a crack of light appeared.

'FIVE!'

The crack of light widened and the ground felt soft under Jamie's trainers as he stepped from the dark cave into Dino World.

Jamie stood blinking in the sunlight as the familiar smells of wet leaves and stinky gingko fruit filled his nose. A moment later, Tom was standing next to him on Gingko Hill.

'Wanna! Here, Wanna!' Jamie raised his voice above the buzzing insects and the calls of creatures in the steamy jungle.

'That's strange,' Tom said. 'He usually comes right away.'

'Maybe we could track him,' Jamie wondered aloud.

Jamie and Tom examined the ground outside the cave for traces of their faithful dinosaur friend and saw fresh footprints—just like the fossilized ones back in the cave—leading down the side of Gingko Hill.

'Wanna's gone south, down the hill,' Tom said, looking at his compass. 'We've never been that way before. Let's follow him!'

'Hang on a minute.' Jamie picked some smelly gingko fruit and put them in his backpack. 'For Wanna when we see him.'

Then the boys hurried down the hill.

'This is steep!' Jamie said as his legs picked up speed.

'Beat you to the bottom!' Tom yelled.

Jamie raced his friend down the hill, skidding and sliding, grabbing at trailing vines and low branches to keep from falling head over heels.

Jamie leaped down the last little way to land in the soft mud at the base of the hill.

Splat!

'I was first!' puffed Jamie as mud slopped over the top of his trainers.

'No, I was first!' gasped Tom. A glob of mud plopped off his curly red hair and splattered onto his freckly nose.

They looked at each other and laughed.

'Shh!' said Tom. 'I can hear a squishing noise.'

Jamie listened for a moment and then whirled round as a wet,

sandpapery tongue
licked his cheek.
'Yuck!' he yelled.
'It's Wanna!' Tom
cheered.

The little green and brown
dinosaur wagged his tail,
splattering mud all over them.
Then he cocked his bony head to
one side and looked hopefully at
Jamie's backpack.

'Here you are, Wanna.' Jamie
handed Wanna a stinky gingko fruit.

The little dinosaur grunked
happily as he gobbled up the fruit,
then he bounded up to Tom.

'Urgh, stinko breath! Aargh!'
Tom landed on his back in the mud
with Wanna on top of him, licking
his face.

Join Jamie and Tom
in Dino World
with the

Turn the page for a taster

of all the awesome

things to do . . .

Create!

MAKE YOUR OWN EDIBLE DINO POO!

YOU WILL NEED:

- 100g plain chocolate
- 50g margarine
- 2 tablespoons golden syrup
- 150g plain digestive biscuits

1. Put the biscuits in a large freezer bag and tie the bag shut. Using a rolling pin, bash the biscuits into crumbs.

2. Break up the chocolate into pieces and put them in a saucepan. Heat the pan on a low temperature until the chocolate has melted.

3. Stir the margarine and syrup into the melted chocolate.

4. Take the saucepan off the heat. Pour the biscuit crumbs into the chocolate mixture and stir together.

Don't forget to ask a grown-up to help melt the chocolate!

36

37

Play!

WHICH CRETACEOUS DINO ARE YOU?

START
Do you walk on two legs or four legs?

Two legs

Four legs

Super speedy or supremely strong?

Super speedy or supremely strong?

Strong

Speedy

Speedy

Strong

Hunt on land or in the air?

Carnivore or herbivore?

Up high or down low?

Protected by horns or bony armour?

Land

Air

Carnivore

Herbivore

Down low

Up high

Horns

Bony armour

T-Rex

Quetzalcoatlus

Velociraptor

Wannanosaurus

Bagaceratops

Edmontosaurus

Triceratops

Ankylosaurus

Discover!

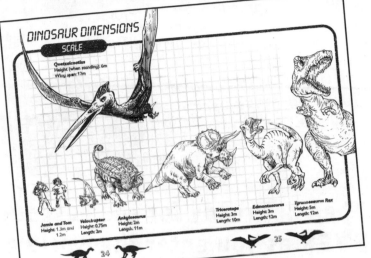

DINOSAUR DIMENSIONS

SCALE

Quetzalcoatlus
Height (when standing): 6m
Wing span: 12m

Jamie and Tom
Height: 1.3m and 1.2m

Velociraptor
Height: 0.75m
Length: 2m

Ankylosaurus
Height: 2m
Length: 11m

Triceratops
Height: 3m
Length: 10m

Edmontosaurus
Height: 3m
Length: 12m

Tyrannosaurus Rex
Height: 5m
Length: 12m

Explore!

T-REX: THE LIZARD KING

Tyrannosaurus Rex was a carnivore that ate all sorts of other creatures, from small dinosaurs like velociraptors to large ones like edmontosaurs. Palaeontologists think the t-rex was probably a scavenger as well as a hunter, eating up the remains of creatures that had already died. With chisel-shaped teeth at the front and huge teeth with knife-like serrated edges filling the rest of its mouth, the t-rex was a fearsome predator. The biggest t-rex skull ever found is 150cm long and was discovered in the 1960s. The biggest and best preserved whole t-rex skeleton is in the Field Museum of Natural History in Chicago. Its name is FMNH PR 2081, but its nickname is Sue.

We found out that competition for food was fierce in the Cretaceous period when we ran into not one but two t-rexes! We'd only just managed to escape one dino's snapping jaws when we stumbled into a battle between two of the massive lizard kings.

Want to join Jamie and Tom's gang?

HAVE HOURS OF FUN
WITH COOL DINO GAMES?

GET EXCLUSIVE
BONUS CONTENT?

ENTER GREAT COMPETITIONS
TO WIN AWESOME PRIZES?

FIND OUT EVEN MORE
AMAZING DINO FACTS?

Then get ready for the best fun EVER as you enter the world of

.co.uk

(t-rex!)

Neath Port Talbot Libraries

1					
2					
3					
4	4/16				
5					
6					
7	1/15				
8					
9					